By CATHARINE F. SELLEW

ADVENTURES *with the* GODS
ADVENTURES *with the* GIANTS
ADVENTURES *with the* HEROES

ADVENTURES
with the HEROES

ADVENTURES
with the HEROES

by Catharine F. Sellew

WITH ILLUSTRATIONS BY STEELE SAVAGE

Little, Brown and Company · *Boston*

LIBRARY OF CONGRESS CATALOG CARD NO. 54–5125

FIRST EDITION

Published simultaneously
in Canada by McClelland and Stewart Limited

PRINTED IN THE UNITED STATES OF AMERICA

TO JOHN

Why the Stories in This Book Are Famous

THE STORIES in this book are old, old stories told many times for many, many years about the great Volsung family. The first Volsung was said to be a descendant of the Norse god Odin. And, because Volsung was part god and part man, he was a great hero with the power to do many unbelievable things. His sons and grandsons were heroes likewise. You will read about their adventures in this book — the saga, or story, people long ago found so exciting that famous artists, writers and musicians painted and wrote about it so that it would never be forgotten.

When you read these stories, you must remember that the long-ago heroes did not think of right and wrong as we do. They thought that they were helplessly caught between the powers of good and evil controlled by the Norns, or Fates — the three sisters who spun and wove and cut the threads of life. They believed that the honor of their name was more important than anything else. To keep their honor they had to avenge any wrongs done to them or to their families. Often terrible deeds were done for revenge — deeds which would be considered wicked today, but were accepted then as fair and right.

A great German musician, called Richard Wagner, wrote four operas based on the Volsung Saga. These operas are called *The Ring of the Nibelung,* and are still given today. The music can often be heard on the radio and on records — played and sung by our greatest orchestras and opera stars. Certain notes and songs make you feel the spirit and ideas in these stories which Wagner turned into musical plays.

Wagner's operas are a little different from the stories in this book because he gave the heroes German names instead of the old Norse names, and changed the plots a little in order to make his operas more dramatic and suitable to the customs of his time. However, if you read the saga as it is told here, you will be able to understand the operas very easily. In the back of the book you will find a list that will tell you how to pronounce the names of the heroes and will also give you the other names Wagner used.

Contents

ADVENTURES
with the HEROES

CHAPTER I

The Sword in the Tree

IN the banquet hall of the Volsungs a crowd was gathering, for it was the wedding day of the daughter of the house. Around the huge oak tree called "the Branstock," the guests awaited the bride. That great tree, growing in the very center of the hall, was talked of with wonder from one end of the earth to the other. So broad was the Branstock that it took five men, arm to arm, to encircle it. It was so tall that its branches, stretching upward, twisted in the darkness of the rafters and pierced the roof, throwing their shadow over the hall of the Volsungs. Under the Branstock the bride, Signy, would meet for the first time the warrior who was to be her husband. Under the Branstock she would marry him.

Laughter and deep voices echoed from the high ceiling. The banquet table was covered with food and drink. The fire roared on the hearth and threw its light on the swords and shields and ruddy faces of the heroes and their guests. Volsung had ten sons and only one daughter. Now that daughter was pledged to marry Siggeir, King of the Goths.

A great shout of greeting arose from the gathering. Signy was entering the hall. How lovely she was, standing there between Volsung, her father, and Sigmund, her twin brother! Her hair fell like sunlight about her face and shoulders. She walked with the same pride and grace of her father and brother. Anyone could see she was the daughter of a Volsung. Eagerly she searched the faces for the one that would be her husband. Where was Siggeir, King of the Goths?

As she drew near to the Branstock, the crowd of guests stepped aside. There against the huge trunk of the tree stood her nine other brothers and one small, shrunken man, dark and glowering. He stared at her with greedy, unblinking eyes. Then Signy knew this was Siggeir and that he was evil. Only

4

Sigmund felt his sister shrink for an instant as she touched his hand, for Signy was too proud to show her dismay. Quickly she smiled and stepped beside Siggeir. If Sigmund had not been her twin and aware of every thought that passed through her mind, even he might not have understood.

But it was too late to change anything now. Volsung had promised his daughter to this man. No Volsung ever broke a promise. Cheers thundered through the hall as Signy allowed herself to be led to her place for the ceremony. She bowed and smiled serenely to those she knew about her. And after the marriage vows had been said, she sat beside Siggeir at the banquet table, laughing with the merrymakers, turning to her new husband with all the respect a good and loyal wife should show.

Suddenly they were aware of a stranger's presence. A man wrapped in a blue-gray cloak strode out of the shadows on silent feet till he stood beneath the Branstock. A great hush came upon the company. The stranger looked neither to the right nor to the left, but stared at the huge tree trunk before him. Those nearest could see his face. He had but one eye! Odin, the All-father, great King of the Gods, had but one eye. . . .

Somewhere in the forest outside a wolf howled. The stranger raised his arm and the shining blade of a sword flashed in the firelight. With one swift stroke, he thrust the sword into the great trunk of the Branstock — thrust it right up to its hilt! Then he turned and faced the company. His voice rang out like a trumpet call. His words were slow and full of meaning:

"The man who can pull this sword from yon tree
Will always be assured of victory."

And slowly he left the hall in the same silent way that he had come.

For a moment no sound broke the spell. Then it was Volsung who first sprang to his feet, words of wonder falling from his lips. Who could doubt that the great Odin had entered the hall of the Volsungs? Gladly he, the head of the house, would give to the bridegroom the honor of being first to try to free the sword. Graciously, Volsung urged Siggeir forward. Signy watched her husband. She saw a flicker

of doubt in his eyes and she knew that he would fail. He had the heart of a coward. Even when he rose to his full height he looked ungrown beside her father and brothers.

The King of the Goths acknowledged the honor given him with a curt nod of his head and reached out for the sword. He pulled. He tugged. He used both hands and threw his whole weight back on his heels. The sword did not budge. He tried again and again, beads of perspiration standing out on his forehead. At last he gave up.

"No one will free that sword!" he muttered.

And it seemed that he spoke the truth. For the mighty Volsung tried and failed. Each of his sons tried, until only Sigmund was left. Would no one budge the great sword? How long would it remain buried in the heart of the Branstock?

Tall and fair, the youngest of the Volsungs stood beside the great oak. For an instant Sigmund's eyes sought his sister's in a silent pledge. Then his hand curled about the sword's hilt, feeling it fit his palm as though it were designed for him alone. With one smooth movement, he drew the sword from the tree

9

as easily as he would from a scabbard and waved it high above his head.

"Hurrah! Hurrah!" shouted the guests. Only Siggeir remained silent for a moment before he too congratulated Sigmund. In that moment, Signy was sure her husband planned some evil. She watched him approach her twin brother.

"What price do you put upon that sword?" the king asked Sigmund. "Name it, and whatever it is, I will pay it so that I may call the sword my own." But Sigmund merely shook his head. Siggeir begged and threatened, but the answer was always the same.

"I pulled the sword from the tree," Sigmund said. "Did you not see how easily it came out? I am sure the stranger meant it for me." Siggeir only scowled and turned on his heel.

"Friend and father of my bride," he said, addressing Volsung: "A month from this great day, will you not let me play host to you, your sons, and kinsfolk? Your daughter will be eager to see you and I shall be eager to honor the Volsungs under my own roof."

Siggeir smiled and spoke so earnestly that who

could doubt his good will? But Signy's heart beat fast with fear. She knew that envy burned beneath the words of welcome.

That night she sought out her father alone.

"Do not come to see us a month from now. Find some excuse, but do not come."

"Why not, fair bride? The invitation was a cordial one. Will you not be glad to see us?"

"Siggeir means no good. Only harm will come to you and my brothers," she said, catching hold of her father's hands in her eagerness to persuade him. Volsung threw back his head and laughed long and hard.

"Daughter," he said when he had caught his breath. "All brides are full of doubts on their wedding night. Go to your husband and forget your foolish fears."

"Very well, Father," Signy said sadly. "But where there is jealousy there is hate. And where there is hate there is evil."

CHAPTER II

Siggeir Traps the Volsungs

FOR A LONG month Signy watched her husband prepare for the coming of the Volsungs. Each day she was more sure than ever that Siggeir planned a trap. When the Goths, armed and ready for battle, began to gather at the castle from far and near, she knew that what she feared was true. What chance would the few in her family stand against this mass of warriors?

Signy stood alone by her window high in the castle tower, watching for the first glimpse of her father's ships. Perhaps she still could persuade him to turn back before any harm was done.

Day after day she waited, till finally, across the line where sky and ocean met, the first mast and curve of sail appeared.

Hastily, Signy threw a cloak about her shoulders and fled down the spiral stairs. Down, around and down she went, fearful that at any moment someone might see or hear her. But at last she was out in the clear air and running free to the shore.

"Please, please turn back!" she cried out to the ships as if they could hear. Only the gulls answered, screaming and mocking her. At last the Volsungs landed and Signy stood once again beside her father and brothers. How tall and noble they seemed — Sigmund most of all, with the famous sword at his side. Then, sobbing, partly with joy at seeing them again and partly because of the danger ahead, she told them of Siggeir's treachery.

"Go back! Go back!" she pleaded. "My husband will stop at nothing in order to get that sword." Volsung kissed her gently.

"My child," he said. "What trouble has come upon you, my only daughter! I wish that it could be otherwise, but we must learn to accept what the Norns have planned for us. The Fates are set in their ways. Never has a Volsung turned backward from sword or fire."

"But the Goths number more than five hundred! What chance have so few of you?"

"It does not matter so long as we die heroes. Never has a Volsung proved himself a coward." So poor Signy watched them unload their ships and gird themselves for war.

It was as she feared. When the Volsungs neared the castle walls they found themselves surrounded by Goths. The battle raged. The heroes fought with all their skill and bravery, but Volsung was first to fall, and soon all ten sons were made captive. Siggeir, like the true coward he was, had remained safely within his castle awaiting the arrival of his enemies, whom he knew would soon be his prisoners. One by one the mighty Volsungs were dragged, bound and gagged, before him. Signy stood by her husband, wild with anger.

"They're of my own flesh and blood, the brothers I hold dear. You have already slain my father. If you love me, your wife, please let them return to their homeland." Tears ran down her cheeks as she knelt before Siggeir. "What harm have they ever done you? Now you have taken Sigmund's sword,

what more do you want?" Siggeir only shook his head and commanded that the Volsungs be chained at their waists to a fallen oak far out in the forest, and left there without food or drink until the wild animals killed them. He ordered that Signy be locked in her tower so that she would be unable to go to them.

Frantically the sister of the Volsungs paced the floor and wrung her hands behind the locked door of her bedchamber. No one approached her except to bring her food. Each day Siggeir would come and tell her which of the Volsungs had died the night before. Each day she dreaded to hear the name of her twin brother. Sigmund, above all the others, she held the dearest. If only she could help him. She shuddered at the thought of him alone and helpless in the dark of the forest, listening — listening to the sounds of wild creatures creeping closer and closer. Signy rattled and pounded on her door. But the sound only echoed in the empty stair well.

Then one day a new maidservant brought Signy her evening meal. Signy noticed the sweetness of her mouth, the kindness shining in her eyes. Perhaps . . .

"You are new here," she said to the girl.

"Yes," the girl answered.

"Are you afraid of the King, my husband?"

"Everyone is afraid of Siggeir, the Goth."

"Would you let me past my door but for a few minutes, if I gave you my word that I would return?"

"I'd be afraid, my lady! Not that you wouldn't keep your word, but that I would be caught. I dare not think what punishment would be mine."

"Of course, of course!" Signy said, frowning in thought. Then she smiled. "But you would run an errand for me?"

"I might, my lady."

"Would you slip out to the forest where my twin brother is chained to a fallen oak? Tell him that I sent you, and spread a thick coat of honey on his mouth and cheeks. Surely that is not much to ask?"

"I could do that. But why? I do not understand." The young maidservant was puzzled.

"Never mind. Do it and I will always be grateful to you. I will see that you are well rewarded."

The maidservant smiled, still wondering about the

strange request. However, she promised she would do exactly as Signy had told her. Signy listened to her light, quick footsteps till they faded away down the stairs. Perhaps now Sigmund could be saved. Wild beasts loved sweets. They would stop to sniff and lick Sigmund's face and give him a chance to wrestle with them and perhaps escape.

The next day the young maidservant said that Sigmund was the only Volsung unharmed and that she had smeared honey on his face as Signy had told her.

"Your brother sent a message," whispered the girl. "He said to tell you that he thought tonight he would be able to set himself free. He understood your plan. He will hide in the forest so that your husband will think that he too has been devoured by a wild beast. When the Volsungs are gone, the king will set you free. Then you must go to your brother in the forest."

"Yes! Yes!" cried Signy, her eyes shining. "You have done well. Your reward will be more gold than you have ever seen. That I promise you."

When her husband brought the news that Sigmund had fallen to the same fate as his brothers, Signy bowed her head as though in wordless grief while her heart sang with joy. Soon she would be free to run to Sigmund. Soon she would discover where her husband kept the great sword. She would see that once again it was placed in the hand of its rightful owner. Then Sigmund would have his revenge.

CHAPTER III

The Broken Sword

IT HAPPENED as the twin brother and sister, Signy and Sigmund, had planned it. Sigmund escaped to the forest and disguised himself as a blacksmith. Every week Signy managed to slip away from the castle and visit him. Always she kept searching for the sword that the one-eyed stranger had driven into the Branstock. Somehow she would discover where Siggeir hid it when he did not carry it at his side. Cleverly she questioned him, careful to make her words seem innocent — the words of a good wife concerned only with her husband's interests.

At last one night, when Siggeir had been feasting and drinking many hours with his friends in the great banquet hall, he called Signy to him and asked her to take the sword, telling her where to hide it.

She could hardly believe her good fortune. Odin's sword was actually put in her hands! Now she could return it to Sigmund. The cruel death of her father and brothers would be avenged.

So she was not really surprised the next night when she was awakened by the wild cry of "Fire! Fire!" The bright flicker of flames leaped on the castle walls. The acrid smell of smoke filled her nostrils. She sprang from her bed and ran past the panic-stricken Goths. Strangely, she was not frightened. A great weight seemed to have gone from her heart. The husband she hated lay upon the floor of the banquet hall, already dead — punished at last for his wickedness. In the doorway stood Sigmund, free from hiding, the sword upraised, the flames throwing a radiant light upon him.

"Hurry, Signy, beloved sister. Hurry!" he shouted. "Only you shall escape from this evil house." But Signy shook her head. Her work was done. She was willing to die, as custom deemed fitting, beside her husband. She would die with a happy heart, leaving her love forever with Sigmund the Volsung.

22

Thus, Sigmund went out into the world alone. Odin's sword once again hung by his side. He grieved for Signy, but he knew that what she had done was right and proper. Now he would find himself a wife and make the name of Volsung ring proudly through the land. But Odin, the all-powerful, had other plans.

In a nearby land there lived a beautiful young princess named Hiordis. Many noble kings and princes sought her hand. Every day they would gather around her in her father's castle trying to outdo one another in winning her favor. But she would smile first at one and then another, saying, "You are so handsome and kind, every one of you. I wish I could marry you all."

Then, one day Hiordis looked beyond the castle wall and saw a horse and rider galloping down the long, winding road. They were coming up to the gates. Who could the rider be? There was something different about the way he sat upon his horse, the way he held his head. Hiordis was no longer listening to the flattering talk about her. She was listening to the shouts of the castle guards, to the answering voice. It had depth and richness. If only the man were worthy of the voice!

After a little, the rider appeared beside her father. She watched them talking together, and then saw them approaching. A queer shiver of excitement ran through Hiordis. This was Sigmund the Volsung. In that first moment she knew that she loved him. It was Sigmund she would marry.

The other suitors, angry and disappointed that a stranger should be the favored one, could only return to their lands. But one man, King Lygni, great ruler of the Hundings, was bitterest of all. He was determined to kill Sigmund and carry Hiordis away with him. For many weeks he was busy gathering his men and provisions. Secretly he armed them and set out in the darkness of night to surprise and conquer the Volsung.

It was early morning by the time the Hundings reached Sigmund's castle. The Volsung and Hiordis were walking outside the walls, enjoying the freshness of the morning, listening to the songs of the birds and talking of the son that was soon to be born

24

to them. A new Volsung was coming to carry on the great traditions of the heroes before him.

Never had Sigmund been so happy. Never had Hiordis looked more beautiful. Her handmaiden walked a little way behind them, always ready to run an errand or help her mistress. Since she had no one to talk to and was politely out of hearing of her master and mistress, she was watching more closely the woods and country around them. She seemed to hear a great deal of snapping of twigs and distant crashing of underbrush. She began to fear the approach of some great animal. And yet, there seemed no real reason to fear. Quickly she caught up with Sigmund and his bride.

"Mistress! Mistress!" she called out. "There is some great commotion in the forest. Would it not be wise to return to the safety of the castle walls?" Hiordis turned quickly to Sigmund, but he only laughed.

"Do you fear even when I am with you?" he asked, putting his hand on the great sword by his side. And the handmaiden was ashamed and said no more. However, they had gone only a little further when King Lygni and his army burst upon them. Sigmund thrust Hiordis and her handmaiden behind some bushes and drew his sword. To the left and right he swung it, felling the men around him; only they kept coming and coming! How swift upon his feet was the Volsung, turning, leaping, dodging! But what chance did he stand against so many?

Then it was that a one-eyed stranger wrapped in a blue-gray cloak appeared in their midst. He reached out and took the great sword from Sigmund's grasp. He lifted it high and struck it with a mighty swing against a rock, shattering it into many pieces. Sigmund's sword was gone, the sword that promised victory! Almost upon the instant, King Lygni pierced the chest of the Volsung. Then, fearing the presence of the one-eyed stranger, and thinking Hiordis had fled back to the castle, the Hundings marched on.

Sigmund, the Volsung, lay upon the ground, knowing that once again Odin had carried out the will of the Norns. Hiordis rushed from the bushes to hold his head against her breast.

"Sigmund! Sigmund!" she sobbed. "They have killed you, and all because of me!" She covered his brow with kisses, tore strips from her own linen and bound them over his wounds.

"My dearest wife," Sigmund held her hand tightly. "It is not you that are the cause of this. It is the will of the Fates. Do not grieve, but listen to me carefully. Soon you will bear my son, the next Volsung. Bring him up wise in the knowledge of all things. Teach him the courage and the pride of the Volsungs."

"But you," sobbed poor Hiordis. "I cannot live without you."

"You must, for our son's sake. I will soon join my father and brothers. Remember that and be happy for me." Sigmund stopped to catch his breath, gritting his teeth against the terrible pain. Then he went on, his voice ever growing weaker.

"Listen carefully, my Hiordis. Gather up every piece of the great sword that lies around yon rock. Guard the pieces well, for when our son is grown the shards shall be forged into the whole. Once again, I know full well, a Volsung will wield that

29

mighty sword — a Volsung, greater than any, to remember what I have forgotten and to do what I left undone!" With these last words, barely whispered now, Sigmund pressed his wife's hand to his lips and died.

CHAPTER IV

Elf, the Viking

WHILE Hiordis wept over the body of her husband, her handmaiden looked nervously about. She, like so many others, had loved the great Volsung, but she feared the return of King Lygni and the Hundings when they discovered Hiordis was not hiding in the castle. Was that a horse galloping nearer and nearer? Was that the sound of footsteps on the path? She stepped close to Hiordis, tapping her mistress gently on the shoulder.

"My lady, King Lygni may return at any moment. We must escape now!" But Hiordis wept on, seeming not to hear, aware only of her grief. A chill wind had sprung up rustling the leaves and blowing gray clouds across the sky. Two black ravens circled slowly and silently overhead. The handmaiden drew her cloak closer about her. What could she say to make Hiordis heed her danger?

"My lady!" she cried again, this time actually shaking her. "You *must* come with me. Remember the son that you will bear. For his sake, come away!" At this, Hiordis raised her head and looked about her through her tears. For the first time she seemed to realize where she was. Sigmund had said, *For our son's sake* . . .

All at once Hiordis sprang to her feet, alert to the snapping of every twig, the flutter of a bird in the bushes, the chattering of a squirrel high in a tree. "Quick!" she called to her handmaiden. "Help me find all the pieces of the sword. Look, there among the stones — and here's the hilt." For a moment she held it to her cheek, crying, "Oh, Sigmund, why did the All-father call you to Valhalla so soon? Are there not heroes enough seated already in his banquet hall?"

But she knew that such words were useless. Who was she to question the wisdom of the great Odin?

Then both the maid and her lady heard the unmistakable beat of horses' hoofs. So close at hand!

Men's voices rang above the sound. For a moment the two women stood looking at each other, blank with terror. To Hiordis, the thought of being carried off by the loathsome Hunding, murderer of her husband, was more than she could bear. Better that he should find her dead beside the man she loved. But then she remembered that the honor of the Volsungs remained with her.

At last a thought — like a flash of lightning across a blackened sky! One hope for escape! Hiordis pulled the handmaiden into the thicket with her and changed clothes, so that the maid became the queen, the queen the maid. Thus disguised, they crouched beside Sigmund's body, ready to be discovered mourning him.

But it was not King Lygni and the Hundings who approached. The Fates were merciful. It was a tall and kindly man, leading a troop of horsemen. Elf, he called himself, King of the Vikings. Who was the slain warrior and who were these women mourning him?

"It is Sigmund, the Volsung," Hiordis and the

handmaiden cried. "Surely you have heard of him, so great was his fame? Sigmund, who from the great Branstock drew Odin's famous sword!"

They sang Sigmund's praises so well that Elf was overcome with wonder. Truly it was a great man who lay dead before him, well deserving of a proper burial. Elf shouted orders to his men, more than willing to honor this hero. He would see that all was prepared in a manner worthy of a Volsung.

All the while he watched with interest the queen and her maid. There was something strange about them, something not quite right. Both were fair of face, but the maid had a regal lift of chin that did not seem in keeping. While the queen . . . What was it about the queen? Was it that she never seemed to know where to place her hands? Elf, the Viking, found himself loving the maid.

The women begged him to take them with him, telling him of their fear of King Lygni and the Hundings. Elf gladly agreed and, as they went on their way, began to question them.

"You do things differently in your land," he said. "Tell me some of your customs. Tell me, fair

U. S.   866788

Queen, how do you know when the hour for rising has come? These winter days are short and there is no light to announce the morn."

The handmaiden, not suspecting the purpose of Elf's question, answered promptly.

"I always have a cup of milk before I feed the cows," she replied with a smile. "So I always awaken thirsty at the proper hour."

Elf nodded solemnly, knowing now the reason he had been perplexed concerning these women. However, he turned to the handmaiden and asked her the same question. Hiordis knew that their disguise was discovered, but she answered haughtily.

"I always know when 'tis morn, because the gold ring my father gave me grows cold upon my hand." Elf took her hand and bowed over it.

"Will you marry me, fair maiden? I promise to treat you kindly. Such beauty and grace as yours will honor my house." Hiordis felt the warm color rise in her cheeks and she looked down at her hands, overcome by the Viking's kindness.

"You honor *me*," she replied gently. "The shelter of your house would be welcome. The kindness of your heart would comfort me, but I have not told you all. Sigmund the Volsung was my husband," and Hiordis told Elf her rightful name and that she was soon to bear Sigmund's son. "No man can I ever love as he, but knowing this, if you still wish me to be your queen, I will."

"Thank you. I will be proud to care for the son of the Volsung as though he were my own." And with these promises, they hurried on to the land of the Vikings.

CHAPTER V

Sigurd's Horse

ELF the Viking more than lived up to his promise to Hiordis. When Sigmund's son was born, Elf fostered the child as if he were his own. He, himself, sprinkled water upon the baby's head and gave to him the name of Sigurd. He was as proud as Hiordis of the remarkable growth of the young Volsung and saw to it that every advantage was given to the hero's son. Every day Sigurd grew more like Sigmund, with the same breadth of shoulder and gallant head. Never was a child so fearless and full of laughter, bringing joy and admiration everywhere he went. How glad Hiordis was that she had lived to bring this child into the world!

But soon Sigurd was old enough to start his education. *Bring him up wise in the knowledge of all things!* — that had been Sigmund's last command. Hiordis repeated these words to Elf, concerned over the great responsibility that lay before her. Elf smiled at the worried wrinkle puckering her brow.

"You need not trouble yourself about such matters, my dear. Here, under this very roof, there lives a tutor schooled in the lore of all men, deft in every cunning save the sword. Sigurd will need no training there, so natural does the feel of weapons come to any born of Volsung blood."

"Who is this man?" Hiordis asked, amazed.

"Regin is his name. So old is he that none can say from whence or in what year he came here to dwell. So sweet are his words that men listen to each one as it drops from his lips. To hear his fingers on the harp is like listening to the music of the gods. He tells wonderful tales of years gone by. He can foretell every change in the weather, understands all of nature's artful ways. He is master of the masters in the smithying craft and, if man can heal the wounds and ills of those upon this earth, he is the one to call upon."

"So great a man has lived amongst us, and I

have never seen him?" Sigurd's mother thought this most strange.

"You have seen him often, but little heed do people give to so pinched and wan a man till they know his true history. He taught me and my father and many even before him. With good faith and free hearts we can trust him with the Volsung's son."

They could not know the danger of placing Sigurd in the hands of Regin, wisest of men. For Regin, who knew all things, was aware of his own fate. He knew the Norns had decreed that he was to fall by a youth's hand. Who could tell but that it would be the hand of the Volsung? Who could tell but that Regin would harm Sigurd in order to save himself?

However, no hint of this came to Elf and Hiordis, and young Sigurd sat many hours of the day listening and learning from the shrunken man, whose small black eyes glittered with all that lived within the greatness of his mind.

So Sigurd spent his days growing and learning all he could, till the time came when Regin, seeing his pupil had reached the stature of manhood, called the youth to him.

"My son," he said. "You have learned well all that I have taught you. You have taught yourself the ways of battle worthy of your name. None can subdue you. Now it is time to go to Elf the Viking and ask him to give you a war horse of your own. When he has granted your request, come back once again and I will have more to tell."

Delighted with this suggestion, Sigurd went at once to his foster father. A war horse of his own! His eyes shone as he swung on his way, the spring of triumph in his step. Indeed, it was a compliment to have the stern and sober Regin acknowledge his manhood.

Elf was more than glad to give Sigurd a horse of his own.

"Go to Gripir, the stud keeper, and choose from his flock whichever steed pleases your fancy," he said with a smile. Regin had done a good job with this tall and handsome boy. And as Sigurd went to the stables, many turned his way. It was a delight to watch him, for all were sure that through his hand great things would come to pass.

After speaking to Gripir, the Volsung strode on across the hill where the stud master had pointed to the Viking's horses turned out to graze.

The day was clear and golden, the sky bright blue overhead. A river plunged swiftly through the fields below, roaring on its way. Sigurd could hear the great steeds snorting and the thudding of their hoofs. From a distance all of them looked fine and fleet, their coats gleaming in the sun. How would he know which would be the choicest one?

Suddenly two black ravens circled close about the Volsung's head and, startled, Sigurd raised his hand to fend them off. Surely, they had not been in the sky a moment ago. Their wings flapped effortlessly against the air. And then Sigurd saw a stranger drawing close. Surely no man had crossed the open field unseen! Such a man Sigurd would not have failed to notice, so strange was he, wrapped in a great blue-gray cloak. A single blue eye looked out from under the hood, and Sigurd heard himself addressed.

"Today you go to choose a war horse worthy of your fighting skill," announced the stranger. Sigurd nodded, finding speech impossible in his bewilderment. "Every one is a mighty steed, but drive them all into the rushing river yonder. Watch them breast the foam, and take the one that fights the tide most easily."

So saying, the stranger disappeared as quickly as he had come. Sigurd stood for a moment, poised on the crest of the hill. He did not have to be told that the All-father's words had advised him, but he wondered for a moment if Regin had known that this was to be. Surely this, and something greater still, was planned for him. What strange tale had Regin yet to tell? The Volsung's heart beat faster, and in that brief moment he pledged himself to do, with utmost strength and courage, any task that lay ahead.

Shouting, flailing his arms about, Sigurd drove the horses into the river. What a sight it was to see, the great herd charging down the steep and slippery

bank, tails and manes streaming out behind. Then
into the rushing water they plunged, heads stretched
high above the swirling foam! The river tugged at
the struggling beasts, doing its best to dash them
against the rocks, but every horse heaved its great
body up onto the opposite bank. How could Sigurd
tell which had done the best? Puzzled, he watched
them shake the water free and wander in the pas-
ture on the other side. Then he saw there was one
that dashed about as though the tussle with the current had merely served to wake him up. Around and
around he raced, swift and sure of foot. This, then,
was Sigurd's answer. This was what the stranger
meant. But Sigurd did not know that this steed
which he chose was a descendant of Odin's eight-
footed horse, Sleipnir. Wondrous was the power
of the Norns!

Having made his choice, and now owning a steed
he could call his own, Sigurd returned to Regin.
But his old devotion and respect for the wisest of
men was now touched with something close to fear.
Not that the Volsung was afraid, but the strangeness

of the happenings of the day made him feel that Regin dealt with powers that could harm as well as help. So he watched and listened warily as he joined his teacher by the fire.

Regin's smile was grim, but satisfied, as he heard of all that Sigurd had done. Then he took his harp, and coaxing music from it with his shriveled hand, began to sing the story of his life.

CHAPTER VI

Regin's Story

HREIDMAR was King of the Dwarfs, the little folk who live in the heart of the mountains and the crevices of the earth. And he had three sons. Fafnir, the eldest, was afraid of nothing, but all feared him — so powerful was his hand. Otter, the second, had great skill with snare and net and could change himself from dwarf to beast to any form he fancied whenever he chose. The youngest son was Regin, not only a master blacksmith, but wise in knowledge of all things.

Now Hreidmar was a greedy man, wanting all manner of riches about him. So, in order to please his father, Regin had built for him a house lined with flashing gems and glittering gold. Fafnir guarded the entrance with his fierce glances and helmet made of writhing snakes. None dared draw near. Thus Hreidmar remained within his gaudy palace, never troubled by intruders.

One day three gods came down from Asgard's heights, dressed as people of the earth, in order to test the hearts of men. One was the great All-father, Odin himself. With him came Loki, the mischief-maker, God of the Raging Fire, and kindly Hoenir, who gave hope to man. Together they wandered through field and forest, looking with interest at man's work, visiting, as travelers, in the homes of kings and servants alike.

After a time they came to wild mountain country where sheer gray cliffs dropped in jagged steps to gullies teeming with water, and scraggly pines stretched upward as though hoping to reach a glimmer of sunlight. Only the fiercest beasts, who hid in caves awaiting their prey, inhabited such a land. But those from Asgard feared nothing and, sure-footed, continued on their way. Loki, always eager for adventure and ever hungry, looked about for some wild animal to feast upon.

Presently they came to a pile of great flat rocks which the sunlight had found. Basking in its welcome warmth lay Otter, Hreidmar's second son. For some reason, best known to himself, Otter often rested in the form of the beast for whom he was named. Thus it seemed that here lay a good dinner for the three gods. Loki promptly drew his sword and slew the beast, flinging its limp body over his shoulders. Then he went on with Odin and Hoenir, hoping to find a place to build a fire and cook the meat.

Soon they approached a great palace from which bright light glowed invitingly. Having no fear of the dread Fafnir, the gods entered, and were amazed to discover that the radiance came from the gold and jewels which lined the walls within. Sure of a welcome, Loki tossed the dead otter upon the ground and turned to Hreidmar with his greeting and introductions.

But the dwarf king did not seem to see the strangers before him. His eyes rested upon the beast flung upon the floor. It was his son! His second son, killed by the gods who thought so easily to disguise themselves. He began to shake, his rage turning him into a terrible creature. His teeth were bared. His fists were clenched and shaken in the faces of the astonished gods. His face was splotched with purple, and the whites of his eyes turned red with blood.

"You have killed my son!" Hreidmar screamed. "You, who come down to rid the world of evil, have killed my son because of your greedy appetite." And before the gods understood what was happening, the king's servants sprang out at them and bound them fast. "Never will I set you free," growled the angry king.

"But it was a mistake! A dreadful mistake, I know full well." Loki, always quick to speak, begged forgiveness. "We had no way of knowing the beast basking on the rocks was a son of yours."

"That does not give him back his life," said Hreidmar bitterly, but there was a sudden gleam in his beady eyes. "Hearken, though, this one chance I will give you. You stranger folk shall be free when you give me the Fame of the Waters, the gathered Gold of the Sea!"

Loki glanced quickly at Odin and Hoenir, knowing they knew how impossible was Hreidmar's demand. The Gold of the Sea, that greatest of waters! The gold that — day after day, night after night, year after year — Andvari, Elf of the Dark, added bit by bit to his treasure pile. None had ever seen it. They could only guess at its wonder. All had heard tell of the great Helmet of Dread and the strange Ring of Gold — the golden ring of Andvari, said to be his magic magnet that drew unto itself all the water's riches. Now the ever-greedy Hreidmar wanted to have them for his own.

"You ask a great deal," spoke up Odin. "Where Andvari hides his treasure, no one can tell. Let us give you all *our* gold. Will that not be enough to satisfy?"

"If it can cover the skin of the otter that was my son, it will be enough," replied Hreidmar with a sly smile. But to their dismay, the gods soon learned that the skin could stretch itself out into an immense size, far too big to be covered by any ordinary treasure.

Somehow Loki must get Andvari's gold. Hreidmar agreed to set Loki free so that he might seek the treasure.

"Listen well, Loki," Odin advised the fire god. "There is a Desert of Dread in the most distant part of the world, where over a well of mountains a mighty water is hurled. None know where it comes from, or where it meets the sea. But in the mist of the spray, in the dark behind the water, Andvari dwells. His work is the storing of treasure within his house of stone."

"Go quickly," urged Hoenir. "Remember our trust is in you. You have always been clever at finding a way to do what seems impossible. Now, if never before, use your quick wits to find the hiding place of the elf and return with his gold."

"And — Loki!" Odin called a final warning. "Do not let your love for adventure get you into trouble. Act wisely. Too much depends on your success."

Hreidmar chuckled, seeming to have almost forgotten his grief over his son. "Watch out, Andvari! You are about to meet your match," he cried, as though the elf could hear. "You'll need all your magic now. It has helped you gather your gold. See that it, too, can help you hold the treasure." Then the King of the Dwarfs turned to the gods with an evil grin. "Now Andvari's greedy heart shall be made to gather and give, or else it will be the end of all of you!"

CHAPTER VII

The Gold and the Curse

LOKI leaped from the evil brightness of Hreidmar's dwelling. How good it felt to be free, racing through the cold dimness of the forest! For a moment he forgot the dreadful importance of his errand. Even the shadows of the wilderness about him seemed to hold no threat of disaster.

But then Loki thought of the great All-father and kindly Hoenir shamefully bound and thrown like captured beasts upon the floor. There they would lie, uncared for, till his return, forced to breathe the foul air of the dwarf king's riches. They could only close their eyes against the blinding glare of the palace walls and even then the heat would burn their faces. Quickly! Quickly! On he must hasten, to the Desert of Dread.

Beyond the wild mountains . . . Beyond the land of mist . . . Along the treacherous twists and turns of mighty rivers . . . On and on hurried the fire god, more swift and sure of foot than any creature of the earth. Always he watched and hoped as sunlight pierced brown waters. Perhaps it would pick up an answering glitter of golden treasure, discover the hiding place of Andvari's hoard. But always he was disappointed.

At last Loki heard a deafening roar, felt a wave of icy coldness rushing through the air. Here the river churned itself into a frenzy. Drops of moisture coated every leaf and branch and rock. He felt the slipperiness of slime underneath his foot. Then he rounded a great gray cliff, and there before him stretched a solid wall of water crashing through what appeared to be the sky. So this was the place where Andvari dwelled! Now to find that evil one and wrest from him his treasure.

It was harder to do than the fire god would have believed. Eagerly he followed lights and shadows behind the water, even plunging deep below the surface, fighting the fierce strength of the currents.

And always the shadows lost themselves in mist and spray. Tired and shivering with cold, Loki crouched upon a moss-covered rock and watched, discouraged, the swirling water spew up the foam. As he gazed, he absently followed the swerving and diving of a great fish.

Suddenly Loki began to think about what he watched. It was a salmon—the largest the god had ever seen. Against the current it leaped, flashing its silvery tail, twisting and slithering through the onslaught of the waterfall. Loki was so close he could even see its eyes. Again and again he found himself attracted by those unblinking eyes. In them flickered a strange intelligence. Could this be . . . ? Surely it was . . . ? Yes! That great salmon was the shrewd Andvari.

As quickly as this thought shot through his mind, Loki knew what to do. Into his pocket he thrust his hand and drew from it the magic net of his sister, Ran, greedy Goddess of the Sea. Across the rushing water he flung it. Once! Twice! But the salmon, warned of danger, slyly evaded the knotted strands of rope.

60

Loki must plan another approach. With dripping net in hand, he watched again as the salmon flung itself into the rush of water. It gave him an idea. Standing in the midst of the river, each foot firm upon a rock, he let the current billow out the net. Then, pulling the ends with both hands, he slowly drew in the great trap. Sure enough, thrashing about in its center was the frantic fish. Loki strained against its weight, tugging steadily. Closer! Closer!

The fish lay limp, caught in Loki's net! The fire god sighed with relief. But Andvari was a sly elf, and just as Loki was about to lift his catch from the water, the salmon did a tremendous flip, rocking the god on his feet. Back and forth Loki teetered, trying to regain his balance. If he fell into the water all would be lost.

However, the young god had not raced so many times from Asgard's heights to the innermost parts of the earth for nothing. His muscles were alert and strong. Bracing his knees as he threw his weight backward, he kept himself from falling, and held fast to the net. Andvari was trapped at last!

In an instant, the salmon turned into a wizened man with shaggy beard. His feet and hands seemed more like the claws of an evil bird eager to clutch its prey. This was the real Andvari cringing in Loki's snare, pretending complete surrender.

"What do you want?" he whined. "Why do you seek out such a one as I?"

"As though you didn't know already," scoffed Loki. "No one needs to tell you anything. Come now, where's the golden treasure? Then I'll set you free."

"Why should you demand my treasure? What claim have you on what I, myself, have gathered year upon year?"

"What is *your* claim, since you wish to bring up the question?" retorted Loki.

"It is mine," said Andvari. "For it is I who have worked to gather riches while others laughed away the day. What more claim could anyone have?"

"The riches belong to others and have come to you by your sly magic!" cried Loki. "Besides, what good will they be, if I refuse to set you free to enjoy them? All the treasure, every last scrap of gold,

62

shall you give to me or never will I let you go!"

Andvari thrashed out against the net's ropes, but only became more entangled. Then he squatted in its center, gnawing at his fingers, his bright eyes glancing hither and thither looking for a means of escape. Loki watched him with a knowing smile.

"Too bad, Andvari! There's no way out. It is better to admit it now, than waste your time thinking up new tricks that will only fail."

"Very well," Andvari muttered. "I can see no other way. Take away this net and I will lead you to my storehouse."

"I have your promise?" asked Loki.

"You have my promise," said Andvari.

So, behind the towering falls, they slipped into a cave, vast and hollow, filled with the sound of dripping water and hissing spray. It smelled of wet earth and things never touched by sun. Loki followed Andvari closely, careful never to let him out of his sight. How easily he could disappear down black passageways, never to return! At last they saw a yellow glow ahead, and soon they came upon a heap of gold the like of which Loki had never dreamed.

Sullenly, Andvari stowed it away into bags ready for Loki to carry back to Hreidmar's dwelling. Loki stood by, pleased to watch the elf struggling to fulfill his bargain. Finally, Andvari tied the last cord around the last sack of gold.

"There!" he grunted. "Take it and go."

"Not yet," smiled Loki. "Not till you bring out the Helmet of Dread and the Golden Breastplate." Andvari's chin jutted out and he bit his lips in anger, but he brought out the helmet and breastplate. As he moved, something jingled in his pocket. Loki's sharp ears did not miss the sound.

"And what is left in your pocket, sly one?" he cried, grabbing Andvari by the scruff of the neck. "Show it to me!"

" 'Tis so small a thing," whined the elf. "Let me keep this one bit to remind me of what was once my own."

"Show it to me!" Loki said again. And as Andvari drew out his magic ring, the fire god snatched it from his hand, picked up the treasure bags, and with mocking laughter raced from the cave.

Andvari stamped his feet and shook his fists in

helpless fury, hurling words of hate after the disappearing Loki. His curse echoed and re-echoed down the dark passageways of the cave.

"That gold
Which I once possessed
Shall to two brothers
Be cause of death,
And to many princes
Cause of dissension.
From my wealth no one
Shall good derive!"

So screamed Andvari, but Loki paid no heed.

CHAPTER VIII

The Dragon
of Glittering Heath

REGIN, wisest of men, plucked a final chord from the harp and sat silently gazing into the dying embers of the fire. Sigurd watched him and waited, sure that his story was not yet done.

> "From my wealth no one
> Shall good derive!"

Regin's voice was scornful. Sigurd was surprised at the sneer spread across the dwarf's face. "As though anyone would heed the curse of one miserable elf!" Regin exclaimed with a laugh — a heartless laugh that held no humor.

It was growing cold. Darkness crept close around them from the corners of the room. Sigurd the

Volsung shivered. There was evil in the air, and once again he wondered at this man who was his teacher. He wanted to jump to his feet, shout at the figure crouching over the harp, hear his own voice ring from the rafters. But still he waited.

"Yes, Loki returned with Andvari's treasure," Regin went on at last, almost as though he were speaking to himself. "And it was barely enough. That otter's skin stretched and stretched till Loki was forced to throw in even Andvari's golden ring to cover it. He had thought, greedy god that he was, to keep it for himself. But Hreidmar's greed was greater still and keen to see that the smallest scrap was not omitted."

Regin suddenly struck viciously at his harp strings. The notes vibrated like the growl of some fierce forest creature, rumbling away into the hollow dark.

Such a mood of hate made Sigurd want to rush away to a place in the sun. But how, then, would he hear Regin's story to the bitter end? The Volsung knew he must stay.

"Fafnir stood by to see the gold, and myself, youngest of Hreidmar's sons. How it glowed, heaped in warm rich piles upon the otter's skin! So bound by its spell were we all that we hardly noticed the stranger folk depart, free to return to the world of their own. Then Fafnir, the fearless one, stretched out his hand to touch the treasure, feel it smooth upon his palm. But Hreidmar would not have it so. No one but himself would touch his gold! Rage boiled up in him. Like a mad man he was, screaming, jumping up and down, cracking his whip wildly about. It should not have been so." Now the climax of the story was coming. Now the reason for Regin's telling the tale would be clear. Sigurd leaned forward.

"Fafnir had nothing to fear. With his great strength, it took little to slay the dwarf king, my father and his! Soon Hreidmar slumped lifeless over Andvari's hoard, and Fafnir claimed it all for himself.

"All for himself!" Regin repeated bitterly. "And why should I not have claimed my share? But wisdom and skill are powerless against the physical strength of the mighty. Out of my home I was thrown, forced to find my way among men. How many years? How long ago? Time is nothing. It does not change a wrong once done. And all the gold is still with Fafnir. He has gloated so over his treasure that he has grown into a horrible dragon. The Dragon of Glittering Heath, he's called today."

Regin's story ceased and once again silence filled the room. A coal snapped upon the hearth, spraying forth a faint flicker of sparks.

"You, Sigurd, my son, can kill that dragon," the dwarf's voice rang out. "You and only you!"

"You speak of me?" The Volsung started with surprise. "Why?"

"Because you, with your splendid youth and skill of sword, have all the strength I have not," explained Regin. But Sigurd was scowling. Quickly Regin went on. "Will you not help a man that is old? Help him avenge his father's death, and win for yourself that treasure of gold that is more than any king of the earth can call his own! Will you not rid the earth of a wrong and heal the woe and sorrow of my heart? Come, Sigurd, surely this much you owe to me, your teacher."

Still Sigurd scowled. All the youth in him, all his love for adventure, cried out to answer Regin's challenge. But he liked not the sound of Andvari's curse. Great wrongs had been done, no one could deny, but Sigurd hesitated at placing the name of Volsung within the shadow of more evil.

"Sigurd! Sigurd!" Regin cried, his voice shaking with emotion. "You cannot disappoint me. Never did I think a Volsung would be a coward."

"Not a coward," Sigurd said slowly. "Gladly I would right your wrongs. But this I say. You must keep the curse. Scoff at it, if you will, but Andvari's words must belong to you alone."

"Very well," Regin agreed quickly with a shrug, his eyes alight with triumph. "That does not worry me."

Then the Volsung leaped to his feet, eager to be on his way. He had waited long for the time when he could set out to do a deed worthy of his name.

"Now, Master of all Smiths," he said to Regin, his voice soaring gaily to the topmost rafters, "forge me a sword that I cannot break and I will be off to Glittering Heath to beard your dragon in his den!"

So Regin set aside his harp and hastened to his forge, throwing wood upon the fire, applying the bellows to the flames. The room grew alive with light and sound, the clash of metals ringing in the air.

At last a sword of shining steel was thrust into Sigurd's waiting hand, and Regin stood aside to watch. Once! Twice! Against the wall of stone, Sigurd struck the weapon. The third time it shattered on the floor.

"Try again, Master. You must do better than that!" laughed Sigurd.

Again the bellows roared, and Regin's hammer smote its mighty blows. Again Sigurd held a sword above his head, feeling the niceness of its balance, the soundness of its hilt. Once! Twice! Thrice! Again the sword split apart upon the ground.

"Master, I'm disappointed," cried the Volsung. "To kill the mighty Fafnir I must have a weapon worthy of the task."

Now it was Regin who scowled, his eyes shifting about the room looking for a solution to his problem. Was the metal faulty? Was his skill to blame? Yet all the time Regin knew the answer. One sword, and one alone, could do the deed. Regin had hoped it would not come to this, but the way of the Norns could never be changed.

Sigurd, too, had remembered.

"My mother," the Volsung said thoughtfully, "once told me of my father's sword. He drew it from the Branstock's trunk many years ago. In his last battle, the sword was shattered by the one-eyed stranger."

Sigurd's eyes narrowed. "My mother gathered each and every piece. Someday, my father told her, those shards would once again be forged into the

whole. That sword is meant for me!" Sigurd shouted with excitement.

"Regin," he said, slapping the dwarf upon the back. "You can forge those pieces, can't you? You can give to me Sigmund's mighty sword!"

Regin surrendered to what must be.

"Bring me the pieces," he said sullenly.

CHAPTER IX

Sigurd Slays the Dragon

SIGURD soon returned with the shards of his father's sword. How happy his mother Hiordis was, to give the long-treasured pieces at last to the son of whom Sigmund would have been so proud! And yet she felt a twinge of sadness, too, for she knew it meant that the time drew near when Sigurd would set out to make the name of Volsung famous once again. She prayed that the great All-father would not see fit to call him to Valhalla too soon. Surely so fine a youth deserved a chance to explore the world under stars and moon and sun for many years to come. Surely it would be as Sigmund had said. Sigurd, his son, would remember what his father forgot and do what he had left undone.

Regin accepted the Volsung's shattered sword and

held the pieces for a moment in his hands. Would he regret restoring so powerful a blade? Would this weapon with its double edge perhaps do him harm as well as good? Still, he had no choice, and with a shrug he turned to his anvil.

Once again the flames leaped high and Regin's hammer fell in ringing blows. Again, and again! It took longer than ever before, but when the dwarf handed the weapon to Sigurd, it lay in shining splendor, more perfectly balanced than any sword the young Volsung had ever held. Like Sigmund's, Sigurd's hand curled about the hilt and felt at home. Swiftly he dashed the blade against the wall of stones, the metal singing true and remaining unmarred, as perfect as before. Satisfied at last, Sigurd, accompanied by Regin, set out to say farewells and begin the long journey to find the Dragon of Glittering Heath.

They rode through mountains which rose higher and higher. The trees grew shorter, the earth more bare of grass and flowers. No longer did Sigurd see the friendly animals of the forest. All was stark and threatening. The wind whipped about them, and, though the sun shone, none of its warmth reached the travelers. Two black ravens, swooping and dipping, were all that could be seen in the vast blue sky. Still, Regin said the way lay farther ahead.

Just as the dwarf began to slacken the pace, a shadowy figure stepped from behind a great gray boulder. Sigurd recognized the same one-eyed stranger who had advised him in choosing his war horse. It was the All-father, come again to give his help to the Volsung son. Regin shrank quickly from sight, but he, too, could hear the words of the stranger.

"Hearken, Sigurd, to what I say," the now familiar voice spoke quietly to keep his words from echoing too far. "Here lies the track where the Dragon slowly rolls his way down to the watering place. Dig yourself a trench in the middle of the path. Hide there within the hole, and wait till Fafnir's body passes above. Then is the time to strike." With this last advice, the stranger was lost amidst the shadows of the rocks.

Regin wisely withdrew, taking with him Sigurd's horse, Greyfell. Fire-bright were his eyes when he thought of his revenge.

"Hurry, Fafnir, foul brother of mine! Drag your loathsome body to your doom!" And the dwarf crept to safety, chuckling with satisfaction.

Sigurd crouched within the trench he'd dug according to the stranger's words. How silent rested the world about him! Only the wind whispered past his hiding place, or was that the breath of the Dragon drawing near? How stiff his knees were growing! The knuckles of his hand about the sword were tensed and white. A branch snapped. A wild cry of some trapped creature pierced the air. Then silence fell again and Sigurd waited.

At last a scuffing, scrunching, slithering sound, a great snorting of breath! Sigurd braced himself and tightened his grip upon the weapon Regin had forged. And then a great wave of heat washed over Sigurd and he saw Fafnir's scales rolling above his head. He thrust the sword deep up to the hilt, and felt the hot red blood burst forth. The Dragon of Glittering Heath writhed and roared and thrashed about. But the deathblow had fallen, and at last the great body shuddered and lay still, stretched endlessly upon the barren ground.

"You have killed my brother, murdered the last of my kith and kin!" screamed Regin, rushing out from his hiding place, apparently shaking with rage. Sigurd stepped back aghast, not believing the anger in the dwarf's little eyes, astounded at the bitter words he shouted.

"But I thought . . ." the Volsung started to protest.

"Thought! Thought!" Regin hurled the words back at him. "You have thought of little else but to kill and call yourself a hero ever since you touched your father's sword."

"But truly . . ." Sigurd tried to justify his deed.

"I demand my satisfaction as kindred of the slain," Regin insisted, baring his pointed teeth and shaking a gnarled finger at the youth whom he himself had led to Glittering Heath.

Sigurd's mind went back to the evil and hate he'd felt so strongly while Regin had told him the story of his life. Then he had wondered at his

tutor, felt some hidden meaning to his tale. That distrust, which he had brushed aside as unworthy, now came out into the light. But the Volsung knew a true warrior never refused satisfaction to those related to the dead.

"Of this slaying you will be free," Regin was saying more calmly, "if you will build a fire, cut out the dragon's heart and roast it for me. Such a heart is full of strength and hoarded knowledge. It will restore to me that which should have been mine long ago. Fail to grant me this courtesy and you shall leave Glittering Heath without honor."

There was no choice, and it seemed small enough a deed where a life might have been demanded for a life.

Seeing that he had won his point, Regin settled himself comfortably against a rock, while Sigurd went about his task. The smile upon the dwarf's face, as he dozed, was shrewd and cunning, but the Volsung was too busy to notice. His mind was too occupied with what had happened, trying to find a reason where there seemed to be no reason.

CHAPTER X

The Ring of Fire

AT REGIN'S orders, Sigurd held the Dragon's heart on a spit over the fire. The light from the flames burned red upon his face. The world about him was silent — a great hush had spread over everything after the echo of Fafnir's horrible death cries faded away. Only the snapping and hissing of the fire and the rattle of the dwarf's breathing broke the stillness. It was as though all living things lay watching and waiting.

Waiting for what? Sigurd wondered uneasily.

He had wrought his old teacher's revenge, rid the earth of a wrong once done; but no glory had he found. With swift attack from his sharpened tongue, Regin had made the deed seem evil — the deed that the dwarf himself had begged of Sigurd. Justice must always be granted to relatives of the dead. And so Sigurd bent as cook before the fire. An unnatural justice it seemed, and not at all to the Volsung's liking. Surely the Norns wove strange patterns into the Web of Fate. He must watch carefully what next he agreed to do.

Absently Sigurd drew Fafnir's heart away from the fire and touched it lightly to see if it were roasted to the proper turn. A few drops of its blood oozed out on to his finger. How hot they were! With a grunt of pain, Sigurd popped the burn into his mouth and tasted the Dragon's blood upon his lips.

Instantly, shrill bird cries filled the air as dozens of the feathered creatures flew out from trees and bushes, drawing near the fire. Without any of their usual fear of flames, they gathered close — birds that Sigurd had missed as he and Regin neared the Dragon's lair. Now they swarmed out of the forest. Several alighted on Sigurd's shoulders, one even upon his head. Others gathered on the ground at his feet, all hopping about and singing excitedly, as though competing with one another for the Volsung's attention. How different their songs sounded! Why, they were singing words — words that Sigurd could understand! What great miracle was this?

"Hurrah! Hurrah!" chorused the birds. "The Dragon is slain and you, our hero, have tasted his blood. Now you can hear what we have to say."

"But I do not understand," said the astonished Sigurd.

"Once the blood of the Dragon passes the lips of any man, he has the power to listen to the language of the birds," chuckled the woodpecker on Sigurd's shoulder.

"Great is the power of the Dragon's heart and blood," croaked the raven, flying low over the body of Fafnir. "Regin has the wisdom to know that. Now comes his time to triumph, and he plans no good for you."

"Who-hooo! Who-hooo!" called an owl from the top of a scraggly pine, blinking yellow eyes at the brightness of the day. "Take heed! Take heed! One chance have you. Kill the dwarf before he kills you."

"But Regin was my teacher," objected Sigurd. "He

88

taught me all I know save dealings with the sword. What thanks is death from one who should feel only gratitude?"

"Haw! Haw!" cried a crow scornfully. "Such service as he did you was for one purpose alone. You, and only you, could kill Fafnir, his brother, who turned into the Dragon because of his greed. Now Regin thinks to take his heart and hoard."

"For some time I have felt a strange distrust," said Sigurd thoughtfully.

"Hurry. Time grows short," hooted the owl. "Eat Fafnir's heart yourself, kill the evil Regin, and gather the Dragon's gold. Then be on your way to do the deeds the last Volsung left undone."

"Hurry! Hurry!" chorused the birds.

Sigurd thought for a moment, but all that the birds had said seemed true. How he had grown to hate the miserable dwarf, his teacher! He glanced at him now, slumped against the rock, a sneer upon his face even in sleep. Sigurd could well believe Regin planned his death. If it was a choice of his life or that of the wisest of men, the Volsung knew what he must do.

Blowing upon the roasted heart till it grew cool enough to eat, he thrust it into his mouth. Then he leaped upon the dozing dwarf and, with one sweep of his famed sword, sent him to join his dragon brother. Now two lay dead upon Glittering Heath.

> "That gold . . .
> Shall to two brothers
> Be cause of death . . ."

Thus Andvari had cursed when Loki had run off with his treasure. But Sigurd had little time to dwell on Regin's tale. Surely the curse could not touch *him!*

The birds flew in excited circles about his head. The Heath rang with their joyous song. Sigurd the Volsung had rid the world of two who had lived only to see evil done. The birds led their hero on to the cave where Andvari's hoard was stored. There Sigurd donned the Helmet of Dread and the shining breastplate, and, loading Greyfell with as much gold as the great horse could carry, he prepared to leave. Turning to go, his eye fell upon the gold ring that Loki had snatched from Andvari in spite of all his pleas. Heedless of the curse it carried, Sigurd stooped and picked it up. He tossed the hard gold disk in the palm of his hand for a minute before he slipped it on his finger for safekeeping — the magic ring that had served the elf so well in drawing the world's precious metals to his door. No happiness would come to those who wore it. That was what Andvari swore. But Sigurd was already listening to more of the strange bird-song.

"Be off! Be away! You are the chosen hero of the day," sang the birds. "Find the ring of fire that surrounds a mountaintop. No man yet has dared to charge through the flames. But he who does will find the warrior maid, Brunhild, asleep, and can woo her for his own."

"A ring of fire? A warrior maid?" Sigurd leaped upon his horse. "Where? Tell me where!"

"Ride on," sang the birds. "Keep your eyes ahead until you see the sky stained fire-red. For you can set the maiden free who has so long been sleeping, punished by her father for grave disobedience."

So Sigurd the Volsung ordered Greyfell forward, galloped down the steep and twisting path. He held his head high, and there was the light of triumph in his eyes as he raced on to do what no man yet had done.

CHAPTER XI

The Sleeping Warrior Maid

LONG AGO, Brunhild, favorite daughter of Odin, defied her father. Once she had been the leader of the Valkyrs — a warrior maid who swept down from the sky upon her white steed, her glittering spear flashing like lightning. Triumphantly she and her army of carefully chosen maidens would descend into the midst of man's battles, to select the bravest heroes, according to the All-father's command.

The battle-maids in their shining armor, with their bare white arms and long golden hair, would carry off the warriors whom Odin claimed. Off to the banquet hall, to Valhalla, they bore them, where all the great heroes gathered in Odin's honor.

But it happened one day that the All-father chose a certain hero, young and handsome, to be brought away from the world of living men. And, as Brunhild watched, ready to obey, her heart softened and betrayed her. It seemed so great a shame to deprive mankind of one so noble and brave, who had just begun to win his way to fame!

"Truly," thought Brunhild. "My father could spare him a few more years. Many fight bravely in this battle who have lived long in the world. Surely one of them will do as well."

So Brunhild, whom Odin trusted above all others, broke her faith and chose a warrior herself in place of the hero her father awaited in his banquet hall.

"Brunhild! Brunhild!" the All-father grieved. "What have you done?"

"Brunhild! Brunhild!" wept her battle-maidens. "What man is worth such disobedience?"

"How could you place your judgment above mine?" Odin wondered in dismay. "What weakness is there within you, my favorite daughter, that you should fail to do as I command?

96

"Go hence!" he thundered in sudden violent anger. "Go to that highest mountaintop and await your punishment."

Brunhild turned with bowed head and did as she was told.

"Farewell, sister! Farewell, beloved Brunhild!" called the Valkyrs, as they watched their leader ride away.

Alone on the mountaintop, Brunhild waited — waited and wondered and hoped for Odin's forgiveness. But when at last he came striding out of the mist, she saw how stern his face was and she knew that she would have to suffer for what she had done.

"Daughter," Odin said sadly, "you know I forgive you because I love you, but never again can I trust you to do as I command. Now your life must be as a mortal one. You must have a husband and serve him as all worldly women are meant to do."

Then Brunhild wept, for she had seen too many men who were unworthy. Some poor wretch might claim her, or, worse yet, a miserable coward, and she would have to humble herself for him. She tried to tell her father of her fears. But he only shook his head.

"One thing I will do to protect you," he said. "After I have stung you with the thorn of sleep — whose sting will last till the man who is to be your husband awakens you — I will command Loki to surround this mountaintop with a ring of fire. So high will the flames leap, so fierce will be the fire's heat, that none but the bravest warrior in all the world will have the courage to pass through. Then you will be assured that no one unworthy can approach." With these parting words, Odin held out the thorn of sleep and watched its sting spread through Brunhild. Slowly she sank upon the ground and stretched out for the long rest to come. Slowly her eyelids drooped. At last she lay wrapped in sleep's great peace. Then Odin turned with a sigh and silently left her.

And as soon as the All-father had stepped below the mountain's summit, a great ring of fire, as high and as hot as he had promised, sprang up around the top and burned there, fiercely protecting the warrior maid who had heard the words of her punishment.

So burned the fire that Sigurd saw staining the sky, making the clouds that hung about the far mountaintop blush rosy red.

"On, Greyfell, faithful steed!" Sigurd urged. "Faster up the mountainside!" And the good horse leaped forward, heedless of the loose stones shifting underfoot. Foam frothed at his mouth and ran down his shanks, but sure-footed as his sire — the great Odin's eight-legged steed — Greyfell did not hesitate on his dangerous way. Along the narrow edges of deep ravines he raced, and up sheer gray cliffs, until at last he brought his master to the very edge of the fire.

Sigurd drew in the reins and patted the horse's wind-tangled mane.

"Here is the ring of fire, just as the forest birds said!" Sigurd spoke aloud. He listened to the roar and crackle of the flames, felt their burning heat upon his face. But neither horse nor rider turned aside. Sigurd tightened the saddle girth, checked the great sword in his belt, then tightened his grip upon the reins and called out, "Forward, Greyfell, through the flames, to free the warrior maid who rests inside!"

On they charged, right into the heart of the flames, and, as they plunged ahead, the fire parted, leaving a path clear for them. Though the flames licked at the horse's mane and tail, glittered upon the Volsung's sword, flared about the Helmet of Dread, they were as harmless as a summer wind.

At last Sigurd and Greyfell were standing upon a barren rock where lay a figure clothed from head to foot in shining armor. Could this be the warrior maid? Sigurd called out to give warning of his approach, but the figure did not stir. He dismounted and walked over to the sleeping form, touched it gently upon the shoulder, but to no avail. Then he carefully unfastened the helmet and let it fall back. In surprise and wonder he gazed upon the beautiful face framed by the maiden's long golden hair. Still she did not waken.

Quickly the Volsung, afraid that some great ill had befallen her, unfastened the rest of the heavy

armor. She lay before him in pure white garments. Then her eyelids quivered, a soft sigh drifted through her parted lips, and once again Brunhild gazed upon the world. First she saw the rising sun and smiled. Then her eyes fell upon Sigurd the Volsung, who stood by, speechless with wonder.

"Who are you?" she asked. But she hardly cared what his name might be. For hadn't he ridden through the ring of fire, which was possible for only the bravest of men? Odin had been kind in spite of all. For, as Brunhild gazed at Sigurd, she fell in love and felt the happiness stirring within every part of her. How good to be awake at last! How good to be alive! How good to love!

Together Brunhild and Sigurd stood on top of the world, alone under the great blue sky. Together they pledged themselves to one another.

"Oh, Brunhild," cried Sigurd. "Hearken while I swear that the sun shall die in the heavens and the day no more be fair if I cease ever to love thee!"

"Oh, Sigurd, Sigurd," answered Brunhild. "Now hearken while I swear that the day shall die for-

ever and the sun to blackness wear, before I forget thee."

From his hand, Sigurd drew Andvari's ancient
ring of gold and slipped it on Brunhild's finger.
Then he took the beautiful daughter of Odin into
his arms.

CHAPTER XII

Visit to the Land of Mist

ALTHOUGH Sigurd and Brunhild had pledged their troth and were filled with great happiness, the Volsung knew that he must bid his bride farewell for a time. Had he not pledged himself, when first he had held Odin's sword in his hand, to right the wrongs of the world, defend the fatherless and oppressed, and do all that his father had left undone? So now he must go forth and seek adventure, to fulfill the honor due the name of Volsung.

"Good-by, Brunhild, my beloved," Sigurd said softly. "Wait for me here, safe behind the ring of flames. Far too long will be the hours that I spend under the sun and moon without you by my side, but when I return, what sweet days will be ours together!"

"Ah, Sigurd, my heart would break if I did not know that you will return, and that we shall spend the rest of our days in happiness. My every thought will be with you on every step of your journey. Farewell, my hero!" And Brunhild stood tall upon the rock, her golden hair blowing back, tears streaming unheeded down her cheeks as she waved good-by to the Volsung. Then the flames circling the mountaintop leaped high once again, and Sigurd was gone.

As Sigurd wandered through the world, he came one day to the Land of the Mist — the Niblungs' land. There he was warmly welcomed by Guiki, their king, for many had seen how well the Volsung sat upon his horse and wondered at the great sword by his side. Few strangers approached their land who were so fair and stalwart, and when Sigurd agreed to accompany them to war, all were amazed at his skill and courage.

"Surely," the Niblungs said to one another, "there is some great and godlike power in this prince who comes to us from so far." And King Guiki urged Sigurd to share their life and pleasures in his castle.

Now King Guiki had three sons and one daughter. The daughter, who was called Gudrun, was gentle and kind, as well as very beautiful. Everyone hoped that Sigurd would fall in love and marry her, for of course they did not know about Brunhild. How sweetly Gudrun smiled upon Sigurd as she served him his meat and wine! How eagerly she listened to every word that he spoke! Quietly and gracefully she moved about, forseeing his every need. The Niblungs watched eagerly, sure that soon the Volsung heart would be touched by such devotion.

But Sigurd, always grateful and courteous, remained unmoved. Often, when addressed, he jumped to attention as though his thoughts had been in another world.

"I cannot understand it," Gudrun's mother, Queen Grimhild, said to the king. "Gudrun is so fair. She has such dignity. And she loves Sigurd so much. You can see it shining in her eyes when she dares to gaze upon him."

"It is indeed strange," replied Guiki. "Yet it is not as though he disliked her. It is only his heart that will not soften. It is too bad. He would make a fine husband and I would be proud to call him son."

Grimhild did not answer. Her eyes were looking far away into some distant place rising from her mind.

"It is only his heart that will not soften," she repeated softly. "I wonder . . ."

Suddenly the Queen of the Niblungs smiled. "My daughter will not have her heart broken because of this hero, no matter how great he is. His heart will soften. I will see to that."

"What do you mean?" Guiki asked.

"I will mix a potion," said the queen, "a draught so powerful that he who drinks it will fall hopelessly in love with the first woman upon whom his eyes gaze."

"Magic! Evil often comes from magic wrought

to change the pattern of the Norns. Be careful what you do," warned the king.

"You!" cried Grimhild angrily. "You and your warnings! Will you sit by and watch Gudrun grow old and unwed? What harm is magic that brings about great happiness? Leave matters of the heart to me."

So Grimhild set forth to gather the proper herbs and brew them into a drink both tasty and potent. Then she poured it into a great golden goblet and gave it to Gudrun, saying:

"Take this to the Volsung. Stand by while he drinks it, and smile upon him." And Gudrun obeyed.

It happened that Sigurd had just returned from a hunting expedition and was hot and thirsty. He was grateful to Gudrun for bringing him this refreshment, and, throwing back his head, drained the cup to the last drop.

Then it was as though he had never known and loved Brunhild. All knowledge of her was wiped from his mind and heart.

"Gudrun!" Sigurd spoke, his voice soft with wonder. "How beautiful you are! The firelight upon your hair shines like wild bee's honey. You have changed since I first came to your father's house." Sigurd took Gudrun's hand and walked with her out into the courtyard. And Gudrun's heart beat wildly, and the color came and went in her cheeks.

Thus, Grimhild's magic seemed to work. All rejoiced as they watched Gudrun and Sigurd together. The Volsung was reluctant to part from her side even for a moment. Everywhere he went, he looked eagerly for Gudrun. Soon he sought out Guiki and asked for his daughter's hand in marriage. The wedding was planned almost at once.

Then, as befitting the great occasion, Sigurd agreed to pledge eternal friendship with Gudrun's two eldest brothers, Gunnar and Hogni. Together the three stepped down into the doom ring where all such solemn rites were practiced. Carefully, Gunnar, the eldest, cut free a circle of sod and placed it upon his shield. Then each man bared his right arm and, with the point of Sigurd's sword, drew forth a few drops of blood which they mingled together

in the fresh black earth. Finally the sod was replaced and together the three stood over it, sworn to true brotherhood — the two swarthy Niblungs and the fair Volsung.

Joyous were the wedding bells; triumphant the cries and shouts of the Niblungs gathered for the ceremony. If a wolf howled in the forest, and the ravens circled overhead, none noticed. If there were a touch of sadness in Sigurd's heart, if strange doubts troubled his mind, he never showed it. The bride whose hand he held in his was too beautiful. Grimhild's magic draught was too potent. But strange are the ways of the Norns and they are never defeated.

CHAPTER XIII

Brunhild Betrayed

"HEARKEN while I swear that the sun shall die in the heavens and the day no more be fair if I cease to love thee!" So Sigurd had vowed to Brunhild. And now he was married to Gudrun, because of Grimhild's powerful magic. Somehow, though Sigurd loved his wife, the days never seemed quite so fair as once in a forgotten time. He missed the sunshine, too. The sun seldom reached the land of the Niblungs, veiled as it was in mist.

"You smile so little, husband," Gudrun said to him once. "Do I not make you happy?"

"Of course, fair one, I save my smiles for you."

"Yes, but when you think no one watches, your face grows sad," Gudrun persisted.

"Your eyes are too keen," said Sigurd, taking his

wife's hand and gazing out of the castle window down into the mist-filled court. "Often I feel a heaviness about my heart. I wonder if I have done as I ought to do. For I pledged myself to serve the world when first I put my hand about this sword." And Sigurd's hand rested on the hilt at his side. "Perhaps I tarry too long in this land of your brothers. Perhaps I am needed elsewhere more."

"How can you speak so!" gasped Gudrun. "Since my father died, my brother Gunnar has depended on you. And my mother and younger brothers turn to you likewise. Think, too, how many you have helped with your strength and kindness. Your name is spoken with love and pride throughout the land."

Sigurd smiled at his wife. Then he kissed her on her forehead and turned away, the troubled frown again upon his face.

Thus it was that the Volsung gladly agreed to go on the adventure Gunnar proposed the following day.

"All say that I should find myself a wife," the new king of the Niblungs said. "My mother sug-

gests Brunhild, the warrior maiden who is surrounded by a ring of flames upon a far mountaintop.
She and she alone, they say, is worthy to become
Queen of the Niblungs. Will you go with me while I
woo her, noble brother?" Gunnar asked of Sigurd.
"For you know," he explained, "she was vowed to
marry whoever has the courage to ride through the
leaping flames."

"Brunhild!" Sigurd let the name rest upon his
lips. "All have heard tell of her," he said slowly.
"That must be why the name rings so familiarly.
Of course I will accompany you on your journey."
And Sigurd's face lit up, welcoming this chance to
find something new with which to occupy his mind.

So they rode together — the pride of the Volsungs and the King of the Niblungs, who were
sworn to brotherhood. Together they ascended the
steep and treacherous trail to the far mountaintop
where Brunhild awaited her hero. The fire still
stained the sky with red. The clouds still blushed
with its rosy glow. And Sigurd wondered why each
unexpected twist and turn seemed so familiar. Even
Greyfell seemed to know where to step with no

touch upon the reins to guide him. But, by now, Sigurd had learned not to question the way of the Fates.

They reached the fire ring and drew their horses to a halt, well back from the heat of the flames. Silently they watched the leaping, flickering light. Then, Gunnar tightened his reins and hugged the sides of his steed with his knees.

"A quick dash, so swift that the flames will hardly know we've passed!" he cried. "That will be the trick of it. Wish me luck, Sigurd."

"Ah, Gunnar," replied Sigurd, who knew not what he said. "You know that I do that. May the gods look kindly upon you."

Forward charged horse and rider, straight for the crimson flames, but, just as they reached them, the horse reared and turned away. Gunnar let out a great oath and dug his spurs into his steed, forcing him to turn back. Once again they made for the ring of fire. And again the poor horse reared and flailed the air with his great forefeet, his eyes wild with terror. It was no use. Gunnar rode back to Sigurd.

"I see your faithful Greyfell does not shun the fire," Gunnar remarked.

"It does not seem to bother him," agreed Sigurd. "Why do you not ride *him* through the flames?" This seemed like a good plan, and the two warriors exchanged horses. But Greyfell did not appear to like any one other than the Volsung upon his back. He tossed his head and pawed the ground uneasily. And, when the Niblung drove him up to the fire, he balked just as Gunnar's own horse had and no amount of threats or coaxing could make him budge. Even Sigurd urged the horse forward, but, so long as Gunnar sat in the saddle, he stood as though frozen to the ground.

Finally the two men led their horses to the coolness of the rocks below the summit, and stood together, bent on thinking of a plan to get Gunnar through the ring of flames.

Then the Niblung remembered a draught his mother, Grimhild, had mixed to carry with him in case of need. Its magic powers could change the appearance of anyone who drank it.

"Sigurd, I know not if I should ask this of you."

Gunnar spoke slowly. "But perhaps, if you rode Greyfell through the flames, you could win the warrior maid for me. This potion will make you look as I look and speak as I speak. Tell me, is this too great a request for me to make?"

"Certainly not!" Sigurd answered quickly. "Do you not know that when we pledged eternal friendship, I agreed always to do whatever I could to help you?" With these words he drank every drop of Grimhild's magic liquor and leaped upon the waiting Greyfell. Through the parting flames they raced, as once before in that forgotten time, and sprang out upon the huge gray rocks where Brunhild sat waiting. With a cry of joy she rose to her feet and ran forward, arms outstretched.

But when the warrior — whom she never doubted was Sigurd — hailed her and she saw his face, she drew back with a gasp of horror. A stranger stood before her, as dark as Sigurd was fair. And the eyes that looked into hers were black and bold.

"Who are you?" Brunhild whispered, her voice weak with shock.

"Gunnar is my name, and I have come to claim

you for my bride. I will make you the great Queen of the Niblungs. For you, yourself, have vowed to marry whosoever passed the flames that guard this mountaintop." The stranger warrior reached out to take her hand, but Brunhild turned away, raising a tear-stained face to the cloud-streaked sky. Sigurd, disguised as Gunnar, watched in surprise, for Grimhild's magic wiped all memory from his mind. Truly beautiful was this daughter of Odin, and he was glad to win so fair a queen for his friend. But was she going to deny him his right, refuse to fulfill the promise she had made?

Poor Brunhild silently cried out to her father for help.

"How could any but the bravest hero in the world break through Loki's fire? Who else but Sigurd can make so great a claim? I have been betrayed!" And she clasped the hand that wore Andvari's ring upon it — the ring that Sigurd the Volsung had slipped upon her finger.

"The day shall die forever and the sun to blackness wear before I forget you." So Brunhild had promised Sigurd, but here stood a man, unknown, to whom also she had made a promise. And a promise made can never be forgotten. She must accept this dark stranger, agree to become his queen. Unless . . . Unless Sigurd returned soon to her. Oh, she must give the Volsung more time, a little more time! Then she looked straight at the man who called himself Gunnar.

"It shall be as you wish," she said to him clearly. "But this one thing grant me. Give me ten days to prepare myself for the wedding. At the end of that time, I will come to your castle in the Land of the Mist."

"So it shall be," agreed the warrior. "To seal your promise, take this ring and remember me." And Sigurd took Gunnar's ring from his pocket. But, before he placed it on Brunhild's finger, he drew off Andvari's ring. It was as the elf had said. No happiness did it bring.

CHAPTER XIV

Sigurd Betrayed

ALONE on her mountaintop, Brunhild waited. Each day she awakened sure that Sigurd the Volsung would return with the rising sun. Each day she was doomed to disappointment. Soon she would have to leave for the Land of the Mist and marry the man who called himself Gunnar. Was there no escape?

"Oh, Sigurd! Sigurd!" Brunhild cried out to the empty sky. "Hurry back to me, for I made a promise and only you can save me from having to grant it to a stranger! It was you who *first* rode through these flames! Come back and claim your rightful bride!" But her cry died away into nothingness, and the ring of fire burned on and the days passed, one by one.

On the tenth day from the time that the strange warrior had appeared, Brunhild had no choice but to prepare herself to become the Queen of the Niblungs. Never would her heart belong to any but the fair Volsung, but in all else she was honor bound to the dark man who had also braved Loki's fire ring.

"How — tell me, Father — how can there be two with the same courage?" cried Odin's daughter in despair, as she left for the Niblung's land. But the All-father gave no answer. The Norns wove the patterns of life.

Gunnar joyously greeted Brunhild at the great entrance of his castle. With pride he led her before the waiting guests, who looked with amazement at the tall daughter of the gods, so radiant in her golden beauty. Indeed, Gunnar had won a queen more than worthy of his name. And, if there was a sadness in her face and if her smile was a little stiff, no one noticed, so overwhelmed were they by her presence.

Down the long vaulted hall they passed to the daïs at the end, where Gudrun and Sigurd sat

125

awaiting them. Brunhild raised her eyes and looked straight into the face she loved so well. Here was Sigurd, sitting beside a woman other than herself! Sigurd, whom she had awaited day after day on her mountaintop!

And Sigurd turned ashy gray and gripped the arms of his chair. For by Brunhild's look, full of sorrow and heartbreak, Grimhild's magic spell was shattered as though it had never been. All his love for Brunhild rushed over him and those few happy days together were remembered at last.

But now Gudrun sat by Sigurd's side and Gunnar claimed Brunhild's hand. Each was promised to another and must keep their vows, locking their secret deep in their hearts. Then the cheers and shouts celebrating Gunnar's marriage beat upon them and they moved as in a dream.

In the days that followed, Gudrun and Brunhild went their separate ways as much as possible while they remained in the same castle. Gudrun knew not why each time she looked upon her brother's queen she burned with hatred, for Brunhild never caused offense. Brunhild tried only to pity Sigurd's wife,

who was innocent of all that had occurred. But when she thought of her in the Volsung's arms she, too, seethed with jealousy. And though she tried to be to Gunnar all that he could wish of a wife, again she failed. For the dark Niblung, so different from the hero she loved, filled her only with distaste and she was unable to disguise what she felt. Gunnar wandered about deep in gloom, not knowing how to please Brunhild, whom he loved more each day.

Only Sigurd went on as though nothing had changed, trying his utmost to still the evil undercurrents that tugged at so many hearts. For, even though he longed for the warrior maid, he knew that far greater deeds remained to be done and that only harm would come from trying to change what belonged to the past.

But Brunhild began to wonder why Sigurd seemed to smile so easily and why he never spoke to her alone, but was careful to remain at Gudrun's side. Bitterness grew inside her and she began to lose faith in her love. At first she had been sure that some black spell had kept Sigurd from returning to her arms. Had she not seen the sudden burst of memory kindle in his eyes? It had all been some terrible trick of the Fates. But now . . .

So it happened one day that Brunhild and Gudrun came upon each other as they both were preparing to bathe in the river that wound its way beside the Niblung's castle. As they stepped out from the bushes and found themselves face to face, all the hate that they had tried so hard to keep well buried rose in them, flashing out in jealous fury.

"I shall go first," announced Gudrun, tossing her head.

"No!" cried Brunhild, rising to her full height. "It is the privilege of the Queen of the land to lead the way. Please step aside so that I may pass."

"To be first is the privilege of the one who is married to the bravest of men," replied Gudrun with a superior smile.

"Then, truly, it is my right still, since Gunnar braved the ring of flames," answered Brunhild.

"Not Gunnar, dear sister. That was really Sigurd, *my* husband. It is time you knew the truth. Sigurd drank one of my mother's magic potions so that he would look like the King of the Niblungs and win you for his friend. Sigurd, and only Sigurd, was brave enough to pass through those fiercest of flames!" And Gudrun's laugh was scornful. Brunhild's eyes burned and crimson color stained her cheeks.

"You lie!" she cried. "You, who have hated me ever since I set foot inside your brother's house. It is this jealousy born without reason that makes you concoct such tales."

"A lie? You call this ring a lie?" And Gudrun drew Andvari's ring from her finger and held it out triumphantly — the ring that held the gold's evil curse! "Was not this ring upon your finger when the man who called himself Gunnar wooed you for his wife?" Seeing it, Brunhild drew back as though it would scorch her. But Gudrun continued to hold it out and went on with what she had to tell. "Yes, you recognize the ring. Sigurd gave it to me when he returned with Gunnar from your far mountaintop. Sigurd told me all. How Gunnar's horse would not ride through the flames. How even Greyfell refused to carry him upon his back. Ah yes, a fine hero you married! Now, step aside, fair Queen, and let me pass."

Brunhild hardly seemed to hear Gudrun's last words. It was as though a great hand had smitten her across the face. For a moment she seemed to stagger. Then she turned and slowly moved away.

"I have been betrayed," she whispered to herself. She could not know that the curse of Andvari's stolen gold had caused it all.

Once back in Gunnar's castle, Brunhild shut herself away, and would not listen to words of comfort from anyone. Alone in her bedchamber, she lay silently grieving while day followed night and night followed day. Finally, Sigurd went to Brunhild to inquire the reason for her grief. She raised herself up and looked him full in the face, and the words of hate and bitterness and heartbreak burst forth as though a great dam had broken, letting all the evil currents free. When the Volsung came out again into the hall of kings, all the sorrow that he had kept hidden so long showed upon his face and his proud head was bowed.

Then Brunhild called Gunnar to her, and he came in to where she had thrown herself upon the bed.

"Husband, you, who have boasted of having the courage to carry you through burning flames, must do one more deed for me if you wish to soften my sorrow."

"Anything, my Queen, anything to prove the greatness of my love," said Gunnar eagerly. Brunhild clasped her hands to her breast and looked far away as though seeking those lost days of happiness. Then she spoke in a voice so low that the King of the Niblungs had to kneel beside her bed to hear.

"Sigurd must die," she whispered. "He has wronged me cruelly and so must die that I may live and face the world without shame." No two men could together breathe in life who both had called the fair Brunhild their wife!

CHAPTER XV

The End of the Curse

"SIGURD must die!"

Gunnar started back in horror at Brunhild's words. He thought he must have misunderstood, but the words she repeated were clear enough and her face remained a frozen mask.

"I cannot bring harm to the Volsung!" Gunnar protested. "You know that long ago we took the pledge of eternal friendship. Surely you do not wish me to betray my sacred promise."

"It matters not to me. All I wish is that Sigurd should die. If you love me, so it must be," said Brunhild in a voice heavy with grief.

Now, Gunnar loved the Volsung well and he remembered the many brave deeds Sigurd had done for him. But Brunhild was dearer still. So he went

134

to his younger brother, Hogni, and told him what must be done.

"But I cannot kill so great a hero," protested Hogni. "I, too, pledged eternal friendship. I, too, love the Volsung well."

So the two Niblungs went to their youngest brother, Guttorm, who had not stood in the ring of doom with Sigurd nor mingled his blood with that of the Volsung in the fresh earth.

But Guttorm refused to do harm to the warrior who had come in good faith to the Land of the Niblungs. Then Gunnar knew he must again turn to the magic of his mother's draughts. And mixing one, he gave it to his brother, Guttorm, all the while telling him of the Volsung's wondrous treasure.

"Ours, all ours, the gold will be, once Sigurd leaves this life," cried the King of Niblungs. "You are not bound by words of loyalty. Why do you hesitate?" And so, while the power of the magic liquor was yet strong, Guttorm took his sword and stole into Sigurd's bedchamber. Twice he saw Sigurd's blue eyes wide in wakefulness, and withdrew afraid. But the third time Guttorm found the Volsung sleeping and pierced him through the heart.

With a great cry, Sigurd sprang up, and, reaching for his father's sword, flung it, with the last of his life's strength, at the fleeing Guttorm, pinning him to the chamber door. Then the Volsung fell back upon the bed to await the time when he would join the heroes in Odin's banquet hall.

Gudrun threw herself upon her husband, wild with grief. Sigurd stroked her hair, and whispered words of comfort.

"Mourn not, for with my death fear leaves your house. Nothing is left to repent. You were caught in the evil web of greed. Now I leave for Valhalla, having done many deeds my father left for me, and given as freely as I knew how."

Brunhild came and stood in the doorway, white and tense, listening to Gudrun's weeping. And, when she heard Sigurd breathe his last, she, too, began to weep for the first time since she had discovered her betrayal. Her tears were like the spring thaw and softened her angry heart till she began to re-

pent of all that she had caused to be done. Some evil of long ago, some wrong brought about before Sigurd the Volsung had ever walked the earth, had guided the busy hands of the Norns. Sigurd and his sword had been sent to right that wrong, and, all along the way, the innocent had suffered to exact the justice necessary to strike out the old evil.

Brunhild, favorite daughter of Odin, turned away, and in her chambers she refreshed herself and put on her most beautiful clothes. Then, lying upon her couch, she drove a dagger into her heart and cried out for Gunnar.

"Husband," she said when he rushed to her side. "I am leaving you now, for never can I love any other but the Volsung. You have loved the best that you knew how, even unto having a crime committed that you knew to be wrong. For such loyalty to me, I thank you. Grant me this one last thing. Lay me beside my hero, Sigurd the Volsung, who alone braved Loki's ring of flames. Let me go with him into the afterworld. Let me wait upon him in my father's hall. Let me rest, at last, forever by his side!"

So the great funeral bier held not only Sigurd, greatest of men, but the fair Brunhild too. Between them lay the great sword that Odin, so long ago, had thrust into the heart of the Branstock that grew in the Volsung's hall. Once again, Loki's flames surrounded them alone together, protected from the evils of the world.

But Gudrun and Gunnar remained behind, each alone in grief. And with them stayed the gold, the gold of Andvari's hoard, the gold that held the curse.

Now Brunhild had a brother, Atli, who soon learned of his sister's death and demanded some recompense from the Niblungs, for he had heard also of the Volsung's treasure. Gunnar and Hogni persuaded Gudrun to go to this King of the Huns and agree to become his wife. What cared Gudrun, one way or the other, now that Sigurd was dead? She did as they wished.

Shortly after her marriage, Gudrun realized Atli was set upon getting all of the famous gold for himself, and when he sent a ring of hers as a token of friendship to her brothers, asking them to pay the Huns a visit, she knew that no good was planned. Hastily she warned them, and Gunnar and Hogni agreed to hide the gold.

Together they carried the heavy bags to the edge of the river that wound its way about their castle. Together they found a secret spot along its banks and swore an oath that, so long as they lived, they would never reveal the place where the gold was buried. With a tremendous splash, they emptied the treasure bags into the rushing water. Down, then, and whirling outward, the ruddy gold fell forth as a flame in the dim gray morning. And so Andvari's treasure rested upon the river's bottom, hidden by the river's rushing current, unheard, unseen. Then the Niblungs set forth for the Land of the Huns.

There Gudrun greeted them with tears of joy, and there they fought as bravely as any men. Outnumbered, they were taken prisoners and, as they foresaw, held for ransom, the ransom of Andvari's hoard. Both lost their lives because they would not tell its hiding place.

Thus the secret of the hidden gold remained forever with the brothers of the Niblung. So the gold rested, stowed away within the river's depths, till bit by bit the current drew it back to the source from whence it first had come — back to the great fall of water where greedy Andvari dwelled; Andvari, the elf whose curse upon his stolen gold brought sorrow to so many. For truly it had . . .

> ". . . To two brothers
> Been the cause of death
> And to many princes
> The cause of dissension.
> From that wealth no one
> Had good derived."

Names in This Book and How To Pronounce Them

Andvari (Alberich)*	*AND-varee*	The elf who hoarded the gold of the sea
Asgard	*AS-gard*	Home of the Gods
Atli	*AT-lee*	King of the Huns; second husband of Gudrun
Brunhild (Brunhilde)	*BROON-hilt*	Leader of the Valkyrs; daughter of Odin; first wife of Sigurd
Elf	*ELF*	King of the Vikings; Sigurd's foster father
Fafnir	*FAF-neer*	Dwarf turned into a dragon; brother of Regin
Greyfell	*GRAY-fel*	Sigurd's chosen horse; descendant of Sleipnir, Odin's eight-legged steed
Grimhild	*GRIM-hilt*	Queen of the Niblungs
Gripir	*GREE-peer*	Stud keeper of Elf the Viking
Gudrun (Gutrune)	*GOOT-roon*	Sister of Gunnar
Guiki	*GWEE-kee*	King of Niblungs; Gudrun's father

* Names in parentheses are those Wagner used.

Gunnar (Gunther)	*GOO-nar*	Prince of Niblungs
Guttorm	*GOOT-torm*	Youngest Niblung son
Hiordis	*HYOR-dees*	Wife of Sigmund and mother of Sigurd
Hoenir	*HEN-eer*	Norse god
Hogni (Hagen)	*HOG-nee*	Second Niblung son; Gunnar's brother
Hreidmar	*HREYED-mar*	King of the Dwarfs; father of Fafnir, Otter and Regin
Loki (Loge)	*LO-kee*	Norse god of fire and mischief-maker
Lygni	*LIG-nee*	King of Hundings, rejected suitor of Hiordis
Niblungs (Nibelungs)	*NEE-bloongs*	People in the Land of the Mist
Norns	*NORNS*	The Fates or Three Sisters who wove the Patterns of Life
Odin (Wotan)	*O-din*	King of the Norse gods; the All-father, the one-eyed stranger
Otter	*OT-ter*	Dwarf, brother of Regin who was slain by Loki
Regin (Mime)	*RAY-gin*	Dwarf and teacher of Sigurd
Siggeir	*SEEG-air*	King of the Goths; husband of Signy
Sigmund (Siegmund)	*SEEG-moont*	Youngest Volsung; twin brother of Signy; father of Sigurd
Signy (Sieglinde)	*SEEG-ny*	Only daughter of the Volsung, twin sister of Sigmund

NAMES AND HOW TO PRONOUNCE THEM

Sigurd (Siegfried)	*SEEG-urt*	Son of Sigmund and Hiordis
Sleipnir	*SLEEP-nir*	Odin's eight-legged steed
Valhalla	*Val-HAL-la*	Banquet Hall of Heroes of the Slain
Valkyrs (Walküre)	*VAL-kirs*	Battle maidens who carried slain heroes to Valhalla
Volsung	*VOL-soong*	Head of the great Volsung family; father of Signy and Sigmund